Jeremiah Eames Rankin

**The Shakespearean Interpreter**

With memorial words respecting Henry Norman Hudson; an address

delivered before the alumni of Middlebury College

Jeremiah Eames Rankin

**The Shakespearean Interpreter**
*With memorial words respecting Henry Norman Hudson; an address delivered*
*before the alumni of Middlebury College*

ISBN/EAN: 9783337412852

Printed in Europe, USA, Canada, Australia, Japan

Cover: Foto ©Andreas Hilbeck / pixelio.de

More available books at **www.hansebooks.com**

THE

# SHAKESPEAREAN INTERPRETER

*WITH MEMORIAL WORDS RESPECTING*
*HENRY NORMAN HUDSON,*

# AN ADDRESS

DELIVERED BEFORE THE ALUMNI OF MIDDLEBURY
COLLEGE BY J. E. RANKIN, D. D.

---

MIDDLEBURY, VERMONT
1886.

# ADDRESS.

E VERY creator needs an interpreter. Indeed, the difference between a creation and a commodity; between a thing that is born and a thing that is manufactured, lies right here : the first can be interpreted, its clew can be found, its fundamental principle can be reached ; you can cut through into its germ, and show it in embryo, the last can be pulled to pieces, till you name and count all its dead parts, and leave them dead as they were. In schools, the pupil is taught structural botany; how to analyze flowers ; that is, how to find the stamens and pistil, the corolla and calyx; a purely mechanical separation of these fragile structures into their constituent members, as though they were put together by hand on a stem of wire ; were made of paper or wax. God's flowers, the buttercups and daisies that toss in the fields, are creations ; the flowers that toss with toss of pride or grace upon the hats of ladies, are commodities.

In Wilhelm Meister, you remember how the great Gœthe describes the attempt of the hero, to act the character of Hamlet. He began by approaching it from the outside; by committing to memory the strong passages, the soliloquies; those outbursts which seemed most characteristic, most to emphasize Hamlet's peculiarities. What college boy has not spouted, "To be or not to be?"—the question still. Then, he tried to take over upon his own shoulders that load of melancholy, which weighed his prototype to the earth, as young men, who read Byron, conceive themselve to be at war with all the world, and with God who made it, and try to write poetry in that vein, the the vein of Mephistopheles. At last, he hit upon the thought that what he wanted, first of all, was a key to Hamlet himself; to what Hamlet was, before his father's death; to what he was, independent of the command, so strangely and awfully laid on him by his father's ghost; independent of his weak mother, his uncle, guilty and suspicious, the crafty Polonius, Horatio the true, Ophelia the pure. Getting that clew, all the rest was easy. And into this Hamlet that was, he would first throw himself, that he might understand how Hamlet would comport, as, by degrees, he became environed by his new surroundings. Thus Wilhelm's Hamlet came to be the interpretation of Shakespeare's Hamlet; Hamlet seen through Gœthe's oriel window.

In his Pendennis, again, Thackeray has given us Miss Fotheringay, as Ophelia. It is Miss Fotheringay in the character of Ophelia, and not Ophelia herself. She performs, as Thackery describes, with " admirable, wild pathos; laughing, weeping, waving her beautiful white arms, and flinging about her snatches of flowers and songs; with most charming madness"; while, as a corpse she is unequalled, though at the instant when Hamlet and Laertes are battling in her grave, she is looking out from the back scenes to see how her acting has affected Pendennis and the family. She was not interpreting the character. She had been taught to make the most of Ophelia, as she interpreted Miss Fotheringay. Ophelia was the lay figure, on which Miss Fotheringay tried on her attitudes and charms.

The subject which I shall discuss is THE SHAKESPEAREAN INTERPRETER.

No man ever can forget the hour when he read the first page of Shakespeare. The memory of it will go with him to his grave. It marked the beginning of a new era. It was the diet of the gods, the taste of which will never leave his mouth. It gave him something new to live for; it made the world new to him. It was in his boyhood. Perfectly ignorant of the unities and harmonies, nay, of all the rules of dramatic art, and happy in his unconsciousness of it, he reads, for the first time, the ghost-scene in Hamlet; he sees the sentinel-watch interrupted by the apparition of the dead king; he hears Horatio's greeting:

> "What art thou, that usurp'st this time of night
> Together with that fair and warlike form
> In which the majesty of buried Denmark
> Did sometimes march?"

It is not in the power of acting to thrill him as Shakespeare's uninterpreted art has done. "I care not," said Abraham Lincoln, "how Shakespeare is acted; with him, the thought suffices." Richard Grant White is right, when he says, "In reading Shakespeare, the first rule, and it is absolute, and without exception, is to read him only. Throw the commentators and the editors to the dogs. Read no man's notes, or essays, or introductions; æsthetical, historical, philosophical, or philological." Yes, and throw, also, the actors to the dogs. Every creation, whether of God or of man has its own language; its one language. Let no man mouth it over to you; or into your ear. There is only one first time that a pilgrim ever stands in sacred places; ever reads a great author. Of the memories of that first time, he can never be rid; but, in their first freshness, those impressions can never return at all; they can never return except as memories. When Robert Burns wrote in his " To Mary in Heaven,"

> " Ayr, gurgling, kissed his pebbled shore,
>     O'erhung with wildwoods, thick'ning green;
> The fragrant birch, and hawthorn hoar
>     Twined am'rous round the raptured scene:
> The flowers sprang wanton to be pressed,
>     The birds sang love on every spray;"

he recorded an experience never to be repeated. Those hours of first love could never come back again. The emotions of his soul so quickened, he transferred to all inanimate things: to water, woods, flowers, birds. They were alive with this new passion; transfigured by it. At that moment, they all spoke

one language ; pulsated with one life ; they all bore
the burden of a single sacred passion.   The first reading of a work of genius  is like the first sacred passion,
the first hours of pure love.

"I do not remember," says Gœthe, " that any book,
or person, or event in my life ever produced such an
effect upon me, as the plays of Shakespeare.   I could
fancy myself standing  before  the  gigantic  books of
Fate, through  which  the  hurricane of  life was raging,
and violently blowing its  leaves to and fro.   I was so
astounded by their strength  and  tenderness, by  their
power and their peace, and  my  mind  was so excited,
that I long for the time when I shall again  feel myself
in a fit state to read further."

What interpretation, what an interpreter can do for
an  author,  Carlyle  has  shown us,  in  his  article  on
Burns.   He reinstated him into his environment ; into
the soil, out  of which  he  grew, crimson-tinted with
life's blood-hue, like  his  own  daisy ; gave him again
his surroundings, in family, in church, in state, in em-
ployment, in manners ; set him again  among the men
and women of his own period ; took his altitude there,
as things were around him.   If he had  hot  blood, it

flowed in the veins of his red-haired mother, who made his very cradle the nursery of song ; who crooned Scotland's melodies in his ears, while as yet he was an infant. If he revered noble manhood, he saw it illustrated as Carlyle himself did, in a father, of whom Scotland might well be proud if he had been her only product ; who was alike at home at the plowtail and as a king and priest unto God at the family altar. If he despised cant and hypocrisy ; if he ridiculed and travestied his contemporaries, who, like the sons of Eli, called themselves God's elect, and acted as though they were reprobates—desecrated sacred things ; it was because the scourge of small cords had been put into the hands of his genius, by the glaring inconsistencies of church officials around him.

Nearly all of Burns' compositions have a local habitation and a name. What is now called the land of Burns is full of memorials of him ; his name is written from one end of it to the other. Where he was born, and where he died ; the farms he cultivated ; the churches he attended ; his convivial haunts ; the Bible he gave his 'Highland Mary' ; that lock of golden hair clipped on that holy Sunday of parting ; Tam O'Shanter's drinking cup ; the kirk where he saw the witches dance ; the fields, where he plowed up the mouse's nest ; the " wee, modest, crimson-tipped " daisy ; the very farm-yard, where, on the straw, he composed " To Mary in Heaven" ; these make the whole region redolent of the man ; of his genius, his wild pranks, his follies, his untimely exit from life. Nature and life there furnished him all his materials. The little horizon which encircled him in Ayrshire, embraced all his heroes and heroines. He had no

> "—— kingdom for a stage, princes to act,
> And monarchs to behold the swelling scene !"

It was peasants, and peasant-life, which he depicted. His ashes rest in Dumfries' Kirkyard, and the centuries move on their silent course. But, Carlyle has done a master-workman's work for him. They never can move the heart of man away from that sacred shrine. His footsteps still echo there ; his singing robes still trail among the daisies. Ayr, gurgling along its pebbled bed, will always go seaward, talking to itself day and night, as the half-witted talk ; daft with grief for the loss of the poet with his faculty divine, who once trod its banks. Sweet Afton will always mingle his name with its musical murmurs. The stock-dove, the lapwing, the mavis, the laverock ; he has laid imposts upon them all, that so long as they tune their voices in song, his name shall never be forgotten. The primrose shall bloom for him, the bluebell and the gowan. The sweet-scented birks, the hazels, the heather, ah ! he has written his name upon them all : Robert Burns, Poet. Does the hot blood leap in men's veins, as they make their first stand for freedom, they call for

"Scots wha hae wi' Wallace bled !"

Do the oppressed and downtrodden think of mankind as God made it and would have it to be, they chant their way to deliverance with the words

"A man's a man for a' that !"

There is not a joy of man's youth, that he has not caught the tint of it and put it down in his peasant water-colors. There is not a note of life's merriment which he has not echoed. There is not a human grief of which he has not chanted the refrain. If you want a transcript of beautiful home-life ; if you want to see man's nature in its loveliest guise ; if you want to see a picture of filial piety, parental affection, youthful love, patient industry, and true religion all in

one, a *tout ensemble* upon which angels might pause
to smile, go to the pages of Robert Burns.   The Cot-
ter's Saturday Night stands there like a monumental
temple, a mausoleum erected by filial hands to the
memory of a household circle, the members of which
have been translated.   And the Jolly Beggars, Tam
O'Shanter and the Holy Fair, are transcripts of another kind of life, no less real, perhaps even more so
—around him.

   But, there is no outward reproduction and restora-
tion of Shakespeare, through an interpreter, as Carlyle has given of Burns.   Though we know that he
was born in Stratford-on-Avon, we know not the pre-
cise day of his birth.   And between the date of his
baptism, April 26, 1564, and the probable date of his
marriage with Anne Hathaway—who had caught him
by her womanly wiles—something after November 28,
1582, when he had just passed his 18th year, there is
not a single actual fact in his life that has been ascer-
tained.   That he was rashly, if not unequally, yoked
in marriage ; and this, after a youth as wild and rol-
licking, if not as disastrous, as that of Burns, is probable.   That he did not live much at home ; and that

his wife and his business may have united to give him a good excuse for this ; that he spent his years mostly in the great London, where men make no marks that are left behind them, seethe awhile as in a whirlpool of being, and are not ; did his work for a livelihood as unconsciously as though he had been a man set to binding old books, or cobbling old shoes, instead of remodeling old dramas ; this seems, also, true That, without any technical education or profession, he attained a kind of proficiency in all knowledge and every manner of life, drawing all things to himself and his art, as by some instinct ; at home in every character in every pursuit ; seeing men and life in their distinctive aspects, and catching their salient points, as by a kind of intuition ; that being of human life, he lived in a stratum above it, as though a philosophical looker-on rather than a participant in it ; this, also, we infer. Much as he honored England, and his works are a monument to her, there is very little to locate him as belonging to any country, to any latitude, to any clime. What he says of England any other poet, a poet of any other nationality, might have said :

" This royal throne of kings, this sceptred isle,
.    This earth of majesty, this seat of Mars,
   This other Eden—demi-paradise—
   This fortress built by Nature for herself
   Against infection and the hand of war,
   This happy breed of men, this little world,
   This precious stone set in the silver sea."

He wrote for all countries, all latitudes, all climes.

You open Robert Browning and read,

" Oh! to be in England, now that April's there,
 And whoever wakes in England sees, some morning, unaware,
 That the lowest boughs and the brushwood sheaf
 Round the elm-tree bole are in tiny leaf,
 While the chaffinch sings on the orchard bough
              In England—now ! "

Here is an Englishman for you ; a man to whom
every changing month of the year in his native land
brings a new chronicle of beauty ; who lives over in
his memory, even beneath blue Italian skies, the tran-
sitions of nature, as England, " mother England,"
writes them in her calendar ; writes them still for him,
though the vision of them is denied ; who shuts his
eyes and is among them again.   It is true that you
can find in Shakespeare choice word pictures, which
are only English ; as for example, allusions to " blue-
veined violets " and " primrose banks " ; and, now and

then, an outburst, a flight of song, like the very thing
described :

> " Lo, here the gentle lark, weary of rest,
> From his moist cabinet mounts up on high,
> And wakes the morning, from whose silver breast
> The sun ariseth in his majesty;
> Who doth the world so gloriously behold
> That cedar-tops and hills seem burnished gold."

And Shakespeare locates himself in time as belonging
to Queen Elizabeth's period, in such passages as that
one of surpassing beauty in " A Midsummer Night's
Dream ":

> *Oberon.*     Thou rememberest
> Since once I sat upon a promontory,
> And heard a mermaid on a dolphin's back
> Uttering such dulcet and harmonious breath
> That the rude sea grew civil at her song,
> And certain stars shot madly from their spheres
> To hear the sea-maid's music.

> *Puck.*  I remember.

> *Oberon.*  That very time I saw, but thou could'st not,
> Flying between the cold moon and the earth
> Cupid all armed; a certain aim he took
> At a fair vestal throned by the west,
> And loosed his love-shaft smartly from his bow,
> As it should pierce a hundred thousand hearts;
> But I might see young Cupid's fiery shaft
> Quenched in the chaste beams of the wat'ry moon,

And the imperial votaress passed on
In maiden meditation fancy-free."

In that also put into the mouth of Cranmer in King Henry VIII, when the bishop baptizes the infant daughter of Anne Boleyn. But, he is no more an Englishman in England than he is a Dane in Denmark, or a Venetian in Venice; though Schlegel rightly calls the historical plays a sort of national epic, as St. Peter's is to Italy.

The literary interpreter is like the Biblical in this: that if possible he must posit his author; give him the setting which he had in his civilization; reproduce him amid his surroundings. This I have already implied as needful in the interpretation of character. Ewald finds that everything combined, in Judah and Jerusalem, to make Isaiah the greatest Hebrew prophet of the centuries; to give him, as the critic expresses it, " that calm, sunny height which a specially favored mind takes possession of, at the right time, in every ancient literature; a height that seems to wait for him, and when he is come and risen to it, seems to maintain and guard him to the end without intermission, as its proper occupier." Everywhere, Isaiah makes himself known as the regal prophet, in his thoughts, the matter of his orations, and the style of his expression. Such a positing Ewald has attempted for this greatest of the Hebrew prophets ; and such a positing Scherer has lately given to Goethe. Shakespeare finds such a height awaiting him in Elizabeth's time. This forms the basis of all accurate interpretation. Authors are to be interpreted just as their creations are interpreted. It is not Goethe alone who produces " The Sorrows of Werther," but Goethe at such a period in his life, and at such a period in the history of German literature. In his genius, Goethe unfolds like the unfolding of the century plant, year by year, and not day by day ; studying himself and his art, and gathering forces for a hundred years, and coming to full bloom only in his last score ; in a certain sense, moving along with all Germany at his heels, as the pied-piper of Hamelin drew the rats and then the children. And when Goethe reaches his " calm, sunny height," he knows himself as thoroughly as he could know another man ; as Carlyle says, "he is neither noble, nor plebeian ; neither liberal, nor servile ; neither infidel nor devotee ; but a

clear and universal man ! For, to say nothing of his
natural gifts, he has cultivated himself and his art, he
has studied how to live and how to write, with a fidel-
ity, an unwearied earnestness, of which there is no
other living instance; of which among British poets,
especially, Wordsworth alone offers any resemblance."
And as Goethe studied himself, so Scherer has studied him and portrayed him.

To know oneself in one's work as a creator, is not
the highest function of the creator. The function of
reflection is inferior to that of unconscious creation.
This, Carlyle himself has been careful to emphasize
in what he says upon Shakespeare in his lecture,
"The Hero as a Poet"; "Shakespeare's intellect is
what I call an unconscious intellect; there is more
virtue in it than he himself is aware of. His art is
not artifice; the noblest worth of it is not there by
plan or precontrivance. Such a man's works, what-
soever he with utmost conscious exertion and fore-
thought shall accomplish, grow up unconsciously, from
the unknown deeps within him; as the oak tree grows
up from the earth's bosom; as the mountains and
waters shape themselves; with a symmetry grounded

on Nature's own laws, conformable to all truth what-
soever." If Goethe is the universal man, he puts so
much of himself into his work that we can trace how
he became so; under what influences of place, of
teacher, of companion, he developed; how he inter-
wove into his novels and his dramas threads from his
own life in its different stages, and from his contemporaries, even of those in the sacred precincts of personal friendship; we can discern his Strasburg period
and his Weimar period; what was done for him by
travel and by court life; how he felt the influence of
Frederike, Lili, Frau Von Stein, and even his own hum-
bler Christine Vulpius, who taught him also; what he
owed to Karl August, and what he owed to Friedrich
Schiller. Bayard Taylor reminds us that it is the
Margaret of his boyhood that appears at the spin-
ning wheel in his Faust. There is no such material
for such an interpretation of Shakespeare. His work
was not that kind of work. It was done on a higher
plane. His Hamlet, for example, is not a man of
shreds and patches picked up in the course of a short
life at Stratford-on-Avon and a longer one in London;
picked up from observation of this man and that man;

partly himself at one period of his life, and partly himself at another period of his life ; but made only from
humanity.  Hamlet is as genuine a creation out of the
possibilities of humanity, out of the certainties of humanity, in certain fixed conditions, as though he actu-
ally lived there in Denmark, and had his father's mur-
der to avenge.  And that is why, and why only, Goethe
himself was able to interpret him in Wilhelm Meister.
But, Hamlet was not made up, as Goethe made up
his Werther ; half from himself and half from a youth
called Jerusalem, the  son of a  Brunswick clergyman,
who shot  himself  in Wetzlar in  1772.   And Shakespeare did  not  have  to  go  about  apologizing for the
liberties he had  taken with  his nearest friends, as did
the great German.

A man must know human nature as Shakespeare
himself knew it, in order to  interpret human nature
in Shakespeare.   As face answers to face in the water,
so the heart of Shakespeare's men to the heart of real
men, the world over.  Even the  historic characters,
those that are taken bodily out of English history, are
so handled ; are so elevated out of the plane where
they lived and acted ; are put in  such positions and

relations to other historic characters ; have such lights and shadows falling on them, that they cannot be justified, without a philosophy respecting them which is true to human nature. And when, as in the character of Julius Cæsar, Shakespeare seems to be untrue to history, he shows himself true to human nature ; he gives us the Julius Cæsar the conspirators thought they were conspiring against. In Rufus Lyon, George Eliot says : " We may err in giving a too private interpretation to the Scriptures. The Word of God has to satisfy the larger needs of His people, like the rain and the sunshine ; which no man must think to be meant for his own patch of seed-ground solely." The very principle which makes it within the compass of the Shakespearean critic to detect the handiwork of the great dramatist, to know it from the work of any Francis Bacon, as Falstaff claimed to know the Prince, by instinct, is the principle not alone that his style is his own ; his power of phrasing thoughts, as no mere man ever before phrased them ; of minting things into expressions, which bear the impress of his genius, as the coin the impress of the mint from which it falls ; but that there are discoverable great laws according to which he worked, the application of which makes his work a unit; gives it unity, like the unity of God's work in nature; and not only that, brings it into harmony with God's work in nature.

Take, for example, the madness of Hamlet and the madness of King Lear; the one, madness in certain departments of life, with relation to certain men and women; madness in certain compartments of the mind, other compartments being all the more acute; and the other, the utter wrecking of the mind, as when a ship goes to pieces among the rocks; its fragments torn apart and hurried away by every breaker. Study these instances as a physician; as a metaphysician; as a philosopher looking at man merely as a phenomenon; no other such work has ever been done by the art of man. Do you ask, "Did Shakespeare know what he was doing, as we know it?" He knew what he was doing, in the sense that it satisfied all the demands of his genius when it was done. And here is the central marvel of his power, that he did it as though he were not doing it. If Bacon wrote Shakespeare, Bacon knew what he was doing and concealed it till Ignatius Donelly came and ciphered it out. Take the struggle which went on in the mind of Hamlet's uncle, when he tried to pray. All the theological and metaphysical disquisitions, from the days of Thomas Aquinas until now, fail of giving us a better analysis of the difference between the old man and the new man in human nature; between moral and natural necessity; between prayer which is genuine, and prayer that is false; between God honored and God mocked in prayer. Here was the better man trying to bring the worser man upon his knees before God; counting over, as a man counts coin out of his own hand into another man's, as the Jews purchased the innocent blood from Judas, all that it would cost to shift back from that orbit of blackness of darkness, into which his sins had wrenched him, into the orbit of light and love and joy, where God was waiting to absolve him and say, " Depart in peace !"

Emerson has said :

> " The hand that rounded Peter's dome
> And groined the aisles of Christian Rome,
> Wrought in a sad sincerity ;
> Himself from God he could not free ;
> He builded better than he knew ;
> The conscious stone to beauty grew."

This is the way instinct works. It seems to impart

itself to the things done, as though they were given under an unseen law. It has been well remarked by Moulton in his "Shakespeare as a Dramatic Artist," that "It is in accordance with the order of things that Shakespeare should produce dramas by the practical process of art-creation, and that it should be left to others, his critics succeeding him at long intervals, to discover by analysis his purposes and the laws which underlie his effects." The art of the swallow in making the arched walls of its nest under the eaves of the barn; in mixing the mortar out of which it builds these walls, is unconscious. The art of the bee in building its hexagonal cells; the electicism of the vegetable kingdom, as it takes coveted qualities from the earth and distributes them, some to stalk, some to leaf, some to fruit, is all under law; is all done "in a sad sincerity," as if nature could not free herself from her Creator. This is the manner in which mind creates.

Nor is Hamlet any more Hamlet than is Macbeth, Macbeth; than is Othello, Othello; Fallstaff, Fallstaff; Jacques, Jacques. Never for one moment does the man Shakespeare show himself masquerading under some other name. The conscious character grows under the hand of the unconscious Artist. And when we come to female character, that most volatile and ethereal embodiment of God's image, we find the same mastery over sentiment and motives such as sway the heart of woman; we find a gallery of female creations as fresh and unique, as though they had been taken as Eve was, from the very ribs of humanity itself : Portia, the magnetism of whose beauty is thus expressed :

> " From the four corners of the earth they come
>    To kiss this shrine, this mortal-breathing saint;
>    The Hyrcanian deserts and the vasty wilds
>    Of wide Arabia, are as thoroughfares now
>    For princes to come view fair Portia ;
>    The wat'ry kingdom, whose ambitious head
>    Spits in the face of heav'n, is no bar
>    To stop the foreign spirits, but they come
>    As o'er a brook, to see fair Portia ;

Portia, a woman set there, as Mrs. Jameson expresses it, as "cotemporary of the Raffaelles and the Ariostos ; while the sea-wedded Venice, its merchants and magnificos, the Rialto and the long canal, rise up before us when we think of her ;" Juliet, with all the Spring fragrance and color and freshness and fervor of a maidenhood just opening into womanhood ; Juliet, dying as the flowers do, because such fragrance and color and freshness and fervor cannot be perpetuated in humanity, any more than in flowers; Juliet, "all love," as Mrs. Jameson has it : "love itself," blending in her one self "the love that is so chaste and dignified in Portia ; so airy-delicate and fearless in Miranda ; so sweetly confiding in Perdita ; so playfully fond in Rosalind ; so constant in Imogen ; so devoted in Desdemona ; so fervent in Helen ; so tender in Viola ; and exhaling her life for love, as the flower exhales its fragrance ;" Beatrice, with a wit as penetrating as the lance of Saladin, with a tongue as shaɪp and ragged-edged and salt as the East-wind, straight from a watery continent of saltness ; and yet in spite of it all, womanly and capable of being wedded ; and so over the whole round orb of female possibilities.    Richard Grant White says that "Shakespeare is not woman's poet."    No, nor man's either.    He is humanity's poet. And  God made man, male and  female ; and Shakespeare has depicted man, male and female.    The same American critic has said that Shakespeare has written next to nothing in praise of woman ; and, therefore, his home-life must have been embittered by Anne

Hathaway. His gallery of female portraits speaks for itself. To depict woman as Shakespeare has done, is her highest praise. It is not praise that woman needs of poets; it is to be portrayed as she is. And as Bulwer has said, "a woman was the first to interpret aright" how Shakespeare had portrayed woman. It took a woman's genius to do it.

It is the German Heine who says : " The globe is Shakespeare's unity of place ; eternity is his unity of time ; and humanity his hero :" and the English Hazlitt : " It is we who are Hamlet." Yes, and it is we who are all the rest : Falstaff and Lear and Macbeth ; Portia, Miranda, Ophelia. For, all Shakespeare's characters are representative and typical; stand ever after as at the head of their class. Ulrici says, "Goethe is, in fact, the microcosm of his own age and nation." Shakespeare is the microcosm of all ages and all nations ; the poet of the æons, turning over for humanity, pages transcribed from the living tablet of the heart.

If all this is true ; if there is no such thing as interpreting Shakespeare from our knowledge of himself or of his material ; if, again, it is true that he did not draw his portraits from actual models seen without, but moulded them from original materials within, as the silk-worm eats and digests fibres of leaves and makes them into silks; if the interpreter of Shakespeare's men and women is obliged to study them and to make their acquaintance, just as he would study and make the acquaintance of living men and women around him; it follows that there is no more difficult, no more eminent, literary work done than that done by the Shakespearean interpreter. Next to Shakespeare, stand the men who best know how to interpret him. It is not strange, then, that such men as Goethe and Schlegel, as Hazlitt and Coleridge have delighted to sit at the feet of this great master. Where else should such genius sit? The work of interpreting Shakespeare, besides quickening a man's best powers, has all the fascination of living among the noblest and and purest ideals of humanity; while the imagination is led on from delight to delight, as was the shipwrecked Ferdinand in The Tempest, by the music of Ariel; and with much the same thought:

"Where should this music be? i' the air, or the earth?
It sounds no more; and sure it waits upon
Some god o' the island."

It is a world of thought and life, which moves en-
sphered in music. There is the sense of an atmos-
phere of magic, like that which surrounds, as with
his invisible network, all the inhabitants of Prospero's
island. Everything beats with Shakespearean life;
and all things contribute to the triumph of his art.
You are as really insulated to impressions from him as
though set in mid ocean; inarched beneath his skyey
influences, you look up to the constellated handiwork,
in his firmament of thought, as though the world of
his magic were the only real one—as while you study
him, it is.

This work of the Shakespearean interpreter, HENRY
NORMAN HUDSON, the man whom our Alma Mater
mourns and honors to-day, chose as the work of his
life. How real it was to him; how his whole soul
was absorbed in it; how he sucked the sweetness of
it, as the bee sucks the flower, may be gathered from
his own words respecting the Shakespearean characters: " I have much the same life in their society as
in that of my breathing fellow-travellers; with this
addition, that I know sickness cannot wither their
bloom, nor death make spoil of their sweetness; "

closing with a quotation from Wordsworth, which
embraces the thought of the monk who ate his daily
bread in presence of Titian's picture of the Last
Supper :

> " I not seldom gaze
> Upon this solemn company, unmoved
> By shock of circumstance or lapse of years,
> Until I cannot but believe that they,
> They are, in truth, the substance, we the shadows."

That he did his work well may be inferred from the
testimony in *The Literary World* of W. J. Rolfe,
A. M., of Cambridgeport, who has chosen the same
department of labor and is authority in it, and who
attributes to Mr. Hudson's lectures, published in 1848,
only eight years after he graduated, his own first real
interest in Shakespearean study. This is what he
says : " Mr. Hudson's works are, to our thinking,
the best piece of æsthetic criticism on Shakespeare
that has appeared in this country ; and one that will
take rank with the great works of its class in English
and German literature." Let us pause a moment, to
take in what this means : This Cornwall boy, the son
of a Cornwall farmer ; in early life apprenticed to a
coach-maker ; attracted to the halls of Middlebury

college—whose daily morning bell was to him like a trumpet call, a literary reveille ; entering here at twenty-two, with an insatiable appetite for books ; in addition to routine work, giving himself to the study of such books as Butler's Analogy, Plutarch's Lives, and the book next to the Bible the great English Classic, the Works of Shakespeare ; does such masterly work, as the interpreter of the great dramatist, that he is admitted into the society of the great universal man, the many-sided Goethe, of whom it has been said that he is the greatest critic the world has produced ; the dreamy-thoughted, philosophical Coleridge ; the acute and epigrammatic Hazlitt.  Gleaning in the same field where they and others have been before him, he so appropriates and digests their thoughts, he so originates views of his own, that when he dies at seventy-two he leaves a compendium of interpretations and criticisms, new and old, second, probably, to none in completeness and suggestiveness, in delicacy and discrimination, in solidity and value ; thus linking himself and his life to that which can never die.

Nor does Mr. Hudson confine himself to æsthetic

criticism alone.  He studies Shakespeare inductively, as hereafter he must always be studied ; shows us how by the coloring of the different characters, their juxtaposition and relation, they modify and relieve each other ; as for example, how the character of Lady Macbeth is rendered endurable and even attractive and fascinating by the fact that she is ambitious only for her husband ; that promotion is sought as domestic partnership, as we see by what is implied in the words with which he addresses her in the letter apprising her of his meeting with the witches : " This have I thought good to deliver to thee, my dearest partner of greatness, that thou mightest not lose the dues of rejoicing, by being ignorant of what greatness is promised thee ; " as, also, in the soliloquy of Lady Macbeth after the reception of this letter :

> " Hie thee hither,
> That I may pour my spirits in thine ear,
> And chastise, with the valor of my tongue,
> All that impedes thee from the golden round,
> Which fate and metaphysical aid doth seem
> To have thee crowned withal."

But, perhaps, a still more unusual and delicate piece of inductive criticism is his treatment of the character of Ophelia, and her relation to Hamlet's mother. Here is a woman who deserves all of her son's invective, when in answer to her question, What have I done? he says :

> " Such an act
> That blurs the grace and blush of modesty ;
> Calls virtue hypocrite ; takes off the rose
> From the fair forehead of an innocent love,
> And sets a blister there ; makes marriage vows
> As false as dicers' oaths ; O, such a deed
> As from the body of contraction plucks
> The very soul; and sweet religion makes
> A rhapsody of words ! Heaven's face doth glow ;
> Yea, this solidity and compound mass,
> With tristful visage, as against the doom,
> Is thought-sick at the act."

And yet, when at Ophelia's burial she talks of her disappointed hopes, we cannot help feeling tenderly toward her :

> " Sweets to the sweet; farewell !
> I hoped thou should'st have been my Hamlet's wife ;
> I thought thy bride-bed to have decked, sweet maid,
> And not have strewed thy grave."

Says Mr. Hudson : " The queen's affection for this lovely being is one of those unexpected strokes of art, so frequent in Shakespeare, which surprise us by their very naturalness. That Ophelia should disclose a vein of goodness in the queen, was necessary, perhaps, to keep us both from misprising the influence of the one, and exaggerating the wickedness of the other. The love she thus inspires tells us that her helplessness springs from innocence, not from weakness ; and so prevents the pity, which her condition moves, from lessening the respect due to her character. Almost any other author would have depicted the queen without a single alleviating trait. Shakespeare, with far more effect, as well as far more truth, exhibits her with such a mixture of good and bad, as neither disarms censure nor precludes pity. Herself dragged along in the terrible train of consequences which her own guilt had a hand in starting, she is hurried away into the same dreadful abyss with those whom she loves and against whom she has sinned. In her tenderness towards Hamlet and Ophelia, we recognize the virtues of a mother without in the least palliating the guilt of the wife ; while the crimes in which she is a partner almost disappear in those of which she is the victim."

Nor is even Mrs. Jameson more appreciative of Ophelia's character, or scrupulous about her reputation, than Mr. Hudson. This, too, is the result of inductive study. "The space," he writes, "Ophelia fills in the reader's thoughts is strangely disproportionate to that she fills in the play. Her very silence utters her; unseen, she is missed, and so thought of the more; in her absence she is virtually present, in what others bring from her. Whatever grace comes from Polonius and the queen is of her inspiring; Laertes is scarce regarded but as he loves his sister; of Hamlet's soul, too, she is the sunrise and morning hymn. The soul of innocence and gentleness, virtue radiates from her insensibly, as fragrance is exhaled from flowers. It is in such forms that heaven most frequently visits us."

Mr. Hudson was also a teacher as well as lecturer and author. For twenty years he gave instruction in Shakespeare to the young ladies in Gannett Institute, Boston. He also taught in other schools in that region. Above the medium height, thin, wiry, with sharp and angular features; with grey eyes, keen, expressive and penetrating; with a facial expression peculiar and striking; not at all an elocutionist, he stood before his audiences and classes as if charged with a kind of electric light, burdened with a kind of volcanic energy, struggling to find exit in flashes or volumes of expression ; in his own untaught and un-trammeled way, by tones, emphasis and accent, ges-tures, contortions and gyrations, getting for himself the utterance he sought and inspiring his hearers and pupils with his own enthusiasm. If he was positive and dogmatic, it was because he had thoroughly studied every foot of ground on which he trod ; be-cause he took nothing by dictation, nothing for grant-ed. He prescribed no routine work ; he required no especial preparation on the part of his pupils. If they could sit in his presence and listen to his discussions and portrayals and subtle analyses without being moved to personal thought and study, without coming to feel with regard to the Shakespearean world that it was a real one and they were in it ; that Portia and Juliet and Ophelia and Rosalind and Desdemona and Cordelia were their sister women, their companions, their teachers, whose aspirations and emulations, whose joys and sorrows they could understand, then, alas ! routine work would do them no good ; they were past getting anything out of text-books. He took a sin-

cere and deep interest in the pupils he instructed ;
felt toward them a kind of fatherly concern, that they
might get an insight into the great themes he dis-
cussed and thus furnish themselves for literary re-
freshment and education all their lives long ; as though
he were conferring upon them a benefit which they
would some day understand.

Other pursuits Mr. Hudson had followed. In 1849
he took deacon's orders in the Episcopal church ; and
from 1858–1860 he served as rector to a church in
Litchfield, Connecticut. During three years he was
editor of the *Church Journal;* served as chaplain to
the " New York Volunteer Engineers" under General
Butler during the civil war, a part of the time under
arrest ; an episode which his caustic pen has duly
commemorated ; and for a short time was editor of
the *Saturday Evening Gazette.* But . it may be said
that he put the strength of his life into his Shakespearean studies. In 1848 he published lectures on
Shakespeare, in two volumes, the work running through
two editions in a single year ; in 1850–'57, an edition
of Shakespeare, in eleven volumes ; in 1870, " School
Shakespeare" ; in 1872, "Life, Art and Characters of

Shakespeare," a work which embraces all the best results of his study in this direction; in 1881, the "Harvard Edition of Shakespeare," in ten volumes. Besides these he had published, in 1874, a volume of sermons; in 1875, a "Text-Book of Poetry"; in 1876, a "Text-Book of Prose"; in 1878, a "Classical English Reader," and at other times, "Essays on Education," "English Studies," and other works. These all give us some conception of his literary activity and capacity. It is only when we read "General Butler's Campaign on the Hudson," a brochure penned after he had been kept by that doughty general 51 days in confinement without the filing of charges, that we appreciate his power to use strong language, his keen wit, his sharp irony, his overwhelming invective. Here is a taste of it: "You, sir, were simply rioting in the abuse of military power, spurning alike at the restraints of law and the usages of humanity. I never imagined before, what it was for an honest man to find himself stripped of all legal protection, and held in the condition of an outlaw' Indeed, sir, no language of mine can fairly express to you how much I suffered during those long, dreary,

dismal weeks spent in your bull-pen. May God defend you and yours, sir, from such hard-hearted and unlawful inflictions ! I seemed to be left alone and helpless in the hands of a most unfeeling and vindictive man ; that man had discovered himself my personal enemy ; he was armed with military power ; he was capable of any outrage ; there was no sense of honor, no grace of manhood in him ; to be mean was his pride, to be brutal was his pleasure ; he was revelling in the license of assumed impunity ; he allowed no law, nor anything else, to stand between me and his malice. But, much as I suffered from you, and bitter as is the remembrance of your inflictions, I shall not regret them, nay, I shall take comfort of them, provided your brutal savageness, as exercised on me, should work something toward inducing the country to scour you out of her honorable service."

For several years before his death, which occurred in Cambridge, Mass., January 16, 1886, Mr. Hudson's spirit had been mellowing and ripening for heaven. His entire manner and spirit had become changed. The Ishmaelite to some, he seemed now an Israelite to all. Dr. Gannett recalls with great pleasure and

satisfaction his allusion to the old Gospels, in which they both believed, as he was bidding the doctor farewell for the Christmas holidays. He was then very feeble, but felt confident that a few weeks of rest would restore his accustomed vigor. ' Dr. Gannett, however, had a presentiment that his work was done, and that the evening shadows were gathering around him. The night before his death, Dr. Gannett received from him the following note, written with his own hand; probably the last words he ever penned. It reads as follows: " I shall not be able to resume teaching next Tuesday. Nor can I tell when I shall; but will endeavor to let you know in due time. Dr. Marcy is to perform a very serious surgical operation upon me. God help me! And God help us all!" From the effects of the anæsthetic, taken at the time of the operation, which was a difficult and delicate one upon his throat, Dr. Hudson never rallied. Thus he went to the stars; to that celestial harmony to which his spirit had been attuned on earth.

Mr. Hudson married Emily S., the daughter of the late Henry Bright, Esq., of Northampton, Mass., in 1852. She still survives him; as, also, their only

child, a son, who is a merchant in Omaha, Nebraska.

Our Alma Mater has graduated many honored sons. Some of them have worn the judge's ermine; some have walked in the high places of the earth; have stood before kings. They have worn the poet's singing robes. The forum has echoed to their eloquence; the pulpit and the bar. They have borne her name and her imprint into the distant parts of the earth; their feet beautiful upon the mountains, as they have gone the heralds of the Prince of Peace. But when one considers the kind of work he did, the quality of it, and the classes for which it has been done, it is doubtful whether any of her most honored sons have ever accomplished for her what will be longer remembered, or what will rest more as 'an earthly benediction on humanity, than HENRY NORMAN HUDSON. In the alcoves of her library his volumes will stand forever, his best memento, his truest memorial, his most solid monument; the instruction, the inspiration and delight of all who shall resort here. It is enough for him that, as Virgil guided Dante through the realms of the under-world, bathing his face with dew, and girding his loins with a reed of patience, so he shall

take by the hand and lead into the Shakespearean wonder-world, generation after generation of young men and young women, as they stand upon life's threshold, flushed with life's morning, seeking to solve life's mysteries.   It is enough for her.

www.ingramcontent.com/pod-product-compliance
Lightning Source LLC
Chambersburg PA
CBHW022207020726
47496CB00008B/2919